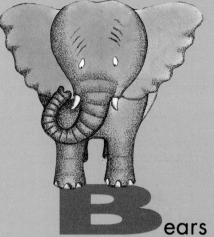

Bears don't go to school. Neither do lions or elephants. Just think— they can't read books like you can! As you read this book, you will find many kinds of stories: some about things you do every day and some about things that are *e x t r a* special. They are all fun parts of

Cover, Introduction, and Title Page Illustrations from *The Little Bear Book* by Anthony Browne. Copyright ©1988 by Anthony Browne. Reprinted by permission of Doubleday, a division of Bantam Doubleday Dell Publishing Group, Inc.

Acknowledgments appear on page 124.

Printed in the U.S.A.

ISBN: 0-395-51916-0

GHIJ-VH-998765432

Bears Don't Go To School

Senior Author
John J. Pikulski

Senior Coordinating Author
J. David Cooper

Senior Consulting Author
William K. Durr

Coordinating Authors
Kathryn H. Au
M. Jean Greenlaw
Marjorie Y. Lipson
Susan Page
Sheila W. Valencia
Karen K. Wixson

Authors
Rosalinda B. Barrera
Ruth P. Bunyan
Jacqueline L. Chaparro
Jacqueline C. Comas
Alan N. Crawford
Robert L. Hillerich
Timothy G. Johnson
Jana M. Mason
Pamela A. Mason
William E. Nagy
Joseph S. Renzulli
Alfredo Schifini

Senior Advisor
Richard C. Anderson

Advisors
Christopher J. Baker
Charles Peters

HOUGHTON MIFFLIN COMPANY   BOSTON

Atlanta   Dallas   Geneva, Illinois   Palo Alto   Princeton   Toronto

HELPING
out

BOOK 1

DO you think helping out
is fun, or hard work?
Sometimes it's a little of both.
Here are some stories
and poems about helpers —
and about some funny things
that happen to them!

Big Book

A PLAY RHYME

Peanut Butter and Jelly

Have you ever made a really BIG peanut butter and jelly sandwich? That's what the boy and girl do in this story — with a little help from their friends!

As you read this book together, use hand motions to act out the words. By the time you're done, you might be hungry for peanut butter and jelly!

CONTENTS

A story from

Punky Spends the Day

by Sally G. Ward

Raking Leaves

Punky put on her coat and ran outside.
"Grampy, wait for me!"

They raked and raked.

Punky worked hard
at being helpful.

Sometimes
the leaves went
into the basket . . .

and sometimes
they didn't.

Sometimes
the leaves went
onto the tarp . . .

and sometimes
they didn't.

They raked for a long time.
"Grampy, I want to stop now."

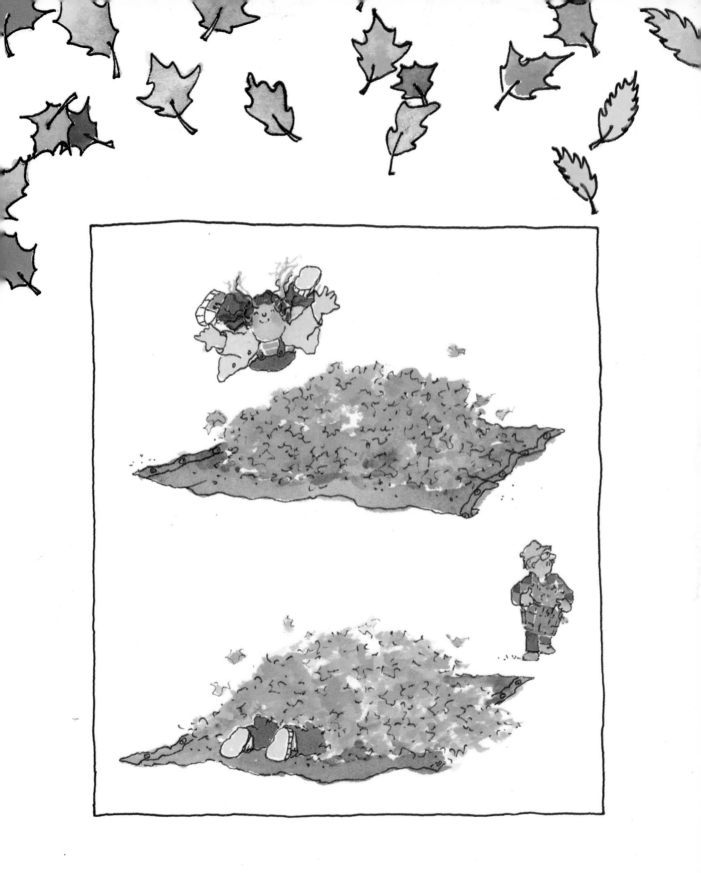

"Goodness, these leaves are heavy!"

surprise!

FUN ways to help OUT

Punky had fun while she was helping her grandfather rake leaves. Can you think of some ways to make helping out more fun?

Make a list of some ways you help out at home or at school. Draw some pictures to show how to make these jobs more fun. Try out your new ideas the next time you're helping out!

Meet the author

Sally Ward remembers how much she liked to hide when she was little, just like Punky! Mrs. Ward is a grandmother now. She has written and drawn the pictures for two other storybooks, *Molly and Grandma* and *Charlie and Grandma*.

The Mulberry Bush

a traditional singing game
illustrated by Ashley Wolff

Here we go round the mulberry bush, The mulberry bush, the mulberry bush. Here we go round the mulberry bush, So early in the morning.

his is the way we dig and rake,
Dig and rake, dig and rake.
This is the way we dig and rake,
So early Monday morning.

his is the way we plant the seeds,
Plant the seeds, plant the seeds.
This is the way we plant the seeds,
So early Tuesday morning.

his is the way we water the garden,
Water the garden, water the garden.
This is the way we water the garden,
So early Wednesday morning.

his is the way we pound the stakes,
Pound the stakes, pound the stakes.
This is the way we pound the stakes,
So early Thursday morning.

his is the way we shoo the birds,
Shoo the birds, shoo the birds.
This is the way we shoo the birds,
So early Friday morning.

his is the way we weed and hoe,
Weed and hoe, weed and hoe.
This is the way we weed and hoe,
So early Saturday morning.

his is the way we shout "Hurray!"
Shout "Hurray!" Shout "Hurray!"
This is the way we shout "Hurray!"
So early Sunday morning.

Here we go round the mulberry bush, The mulberry bush, the mulberry bush. Here we go round the mulberry bush, So early in the morning.

A Helpful Song

Think of some helpful things you could do
for someone. Then add your ideas to the song.
Sing your song the next time you're helping
someone out. Ask other helpers to sing or
whistle along with you. You'll be done in
no time!

A Song from Long Ago

    "The Mulberry Bush" is a singing game from long ago. Back then, children danced in a circle as they sang. Then they acted out the words about each day's work. They often sang about washing clothes and baking bread.

    Today, children like to make up new words. Maybe some new verses will tell about using computers or working in space!

My Dad And I

My Dad and I
made shavings fly:
we built a shelf for books,
and planed a door
and patched the floor
and put up several hooks,
and plugged a leak
and oiled a squeak
and got a toaster wired.
I hoped we might
keep on all night . . .
but Dad got AWFULLY tired.

by Aileen Fisher

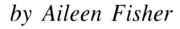

Wonderful
Dinner

I set the table
I made it all neat,
And everyone said
When they sat down to eat,
"The table looks pretty.
You did it just right."

It was a wonderful
Dinner that night!

by Leland B. Jacobs

Everyday Helpers
People Who Help Us Get Our Mail

Did you ever send a letter or get a letter in the mail? How did your letter get from one place to the other? A lot of people helped — that's how! Let's see what happens.

1 You write a letter...

2 and mail it.

3

A mail carrier
picks up all the mail in
the mailbox...

4

and takes it to
the post office.

5

The post office
handles a lot of letters
every day!

6

All the letters have to
be sorted by size.

7 Then the letters are sorted again by zip code.

8

Computers...

9

and other machines...

10

sort the letters
into bins.

11

Each mail carrier has a
special bin. The mail carrier
picks up the mail in the bin
and delivers it.

Now you know about some special
helpers — the people who help us
get our mail.

Sophie and Jack Help Out

by Judy Taylor   illustrated by Susan Gantner

42

Spring had arrived.

But everyone was worried.

Papa could not plant the vegetables.

He was not well.

"I'll do it," said Sophie.

"I'll help," said Jack.

So they dug

and they weeded,

they raked

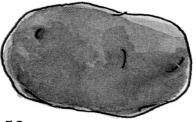

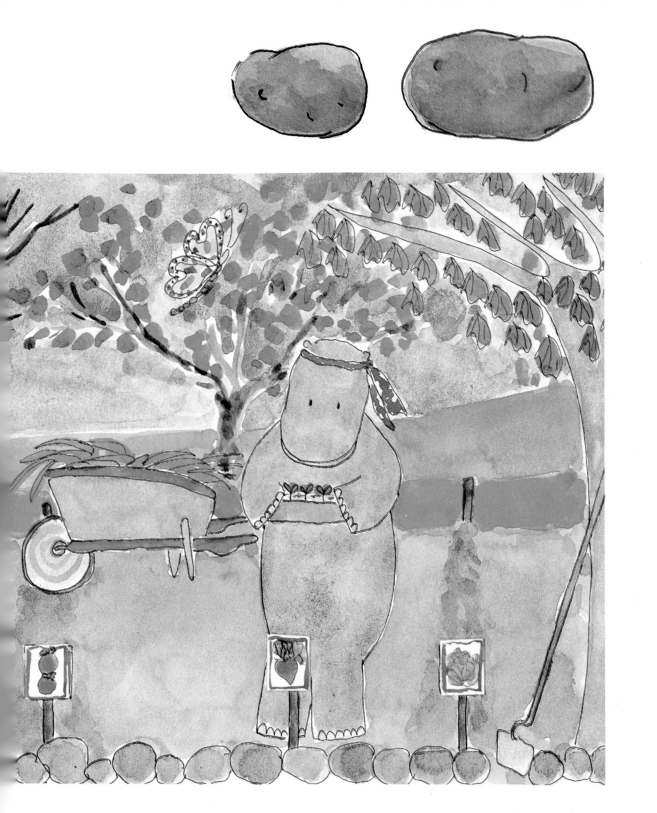

and they planted.

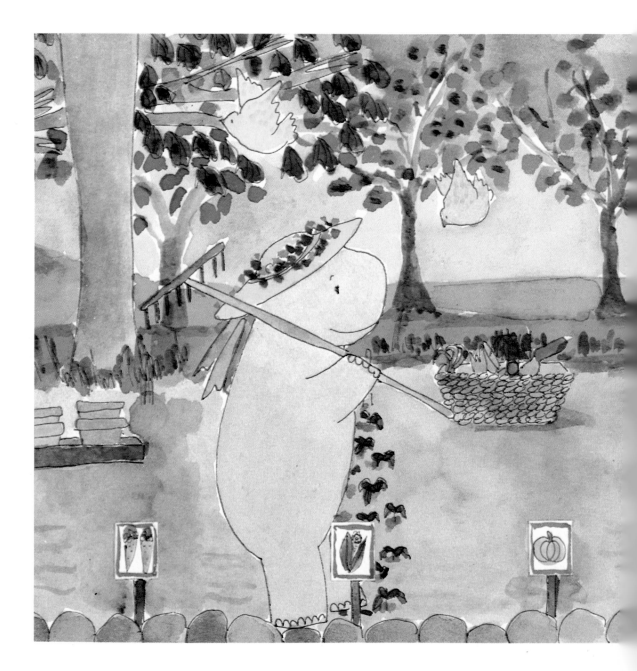

Soon it was all done.

But that night the wind roared

and the rain poured.

The garden was a mess.

"I'll fix it," said Jack.

"I'll help," said Sophie.

When the vegetables were ready

there were many surprises.

Can you see why?

Help Out With Signs

To help find each vegetable, Sophie and Jack put up signs in the garden. Make some helpful signs to put around the classroom. Put your signs up where they can help someone!

DINOSAURS

School begins at 8:15 am.

To borrow a dinosaur book, sign here.

Things I Can Do To Help
1.
2.
3.

How To Take care of plants
1. Water once a week.
2. Keep near sunny window.

Today's Helpers
Erase chalkboard — Gil
Close windows — Mary
Put books away—Jan
Water plants —Pat

Meet the Author

Sophie and Jack Help Out is the second storybook by Judy Taylor. She also wrote a third one, *Sophie and Jack in the Snow*.

Mrs. Taylor is a grandmother now, but she still likes to read storybooks. One of her favorites is *Peter Rabbit* by Beatrix Potter. She likes it so much that she has written three books about the author!

Meet the Illustrator

Susan Gantner studied painting in art school. Today she is best known for her paintings of animals on greeting cards. Sophie and Jack have appeared on some of her cards, but Ms. Gantner also likes to paint pictures of cats and bears.

Some of her cards are shown here.

Help Yourself to Some Good Books

Peanut Butter and Jelly

by Nadine Bernard Westcott

If you liked the chant in this book when you read it together, try reading it again. This time, add your *own* hand motions.

Busy Monday Morning

by Janina Domanska

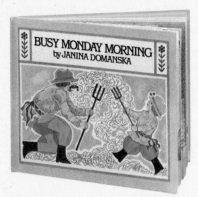

A boy helps his father do something different every day of the week. Sing this song along with them and find out how they get the hay ready for the cows.

Helping Out

by George Ancona

These girls and boys help out with everything from cooking to changing the oil in a car. When you see the photographs, you'll want to be a helper, too!

Growing Vegetable Soup

by Lois Ehlert

What would you do with a garden full of vegetables? Make soup! The recipe is here, too, so you might even try it yourself.

SOMETHING SPECIAL

Do you have something that is special to you? It could be a special friend, a special toy, a special pet — a special anything!

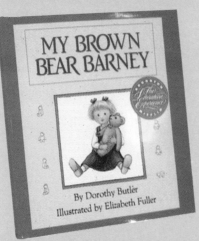

BOOK 2

BIG BOOK

This book is about a girl who takes her special bear everywhere she goes! Read this book together. Find out what the girl does with her bear when school begins.

CONTENTS

If you don't have
a special story yet,
read on! Each of these
stories and poems
has something extra
special in it.

If I had a pig
MICK INKPEN

WITH
CARE

If I had a pig…

I would tell him…

…a joke.

I would hide from him…
…and jump out.

Boo!

We could make a house…
…and have our friends sleep over.

We could paint pictures…
…of each other.

We could have fights…
…and piggybacks.

On his birthday...
...I would bake him a cake.

I would race him...
...to the park.

If it snowed...
...I would make him a snowpig.

We would need our boots…

…if it rained.

We could stay in the bath…
…until we wrinkled up.

I would read him a story...
...and take him to bed.

A SPECIAL FRIEND

Did the boy in this story really have a pig, or did he just imagine one? Would you like to have a pig or some other special animal friend? Write about something that you and your friend could do together. Draw a picture, too.

Mick Inkpen has written and drawn the pictures for another storybook about a special animal friend, *If I Had a Sheep*. He and his partner, Nick Butterworth, have worked on over twenty books together. They also helped produce a children's television program in England called "Rub-a-Dub-Tub."

SPECIAL DAYS

we love a PARADE

FOURTH of JULY

SPECIAL DAYS

HALLOWEEN

CINCO DE MAYO

SPECIAL DAYS

BIRTHDAYS

CHRISTMAS

CHANUKAH

SPECIAL DAYS

Johnny

To Johnny a box
is a house
or a car
or a ship
or a train
or a horse.
A stick
is a sword
or a spear
or a cane,
and a carpet
is magic,
of course.

by Marci Ridlon

My Teddy Bear

A teddy bear is a faithful friend.
You can pick him up at either end.
His fur is the color
    of breakfast toast,
And he's always there
    when you need him most.

by Marchette Chute

Good Books, Good Times!

Good books.
Good times.
Good stories.
Good rhymes.
Good beginnings.
Good ends.
Good people.
Good friends.
Good fiction.
Good facts.
Good adventures.
Good acts.
Good stories.
Good rhymes.
Good books.
Good times.

by Lee Bennett Hopkins

MONSTER CAN'T SLEEP

by Virginia Mueller

illustrated by Lynn Munsinger

Monster was playing with
his stuffed spider.
"It's bedtime," said Mother.

But Monster wasn't sleepy.

Father gave Monster some warm milk.

But Monster wasn't sleepy.

Mother read Monster a bedtime story.

But Monster wasn't sleepy.

Mother and Father kissed Monster
good night.

But Monster wasn't sleepy.

"It's time for bed," said Mother.
"Good night!"

"It's bedtime for Spider, too,"
said Monster.

He brought Spider some warm milk.

He told Spider a story.

He gave Spider a kiss.

"Good night, Spider," said Monster.

Then Monster went to sleep.

HUSH, Little Monster

Can you think of some other special things that might help Monster sleep? Make a list. Then put one of your ideas in this rhyme:

Monster's still awake.
He's tried counting sheep.
Here's a special _____
To help Monster sleep.

Make up a tune and sing a lullaby for Monster. You and your friends might even want to make a Monster songbook!

Meet the Illustrator

Lynn Munsinger drew the pictures for all the storybooks about Monster.

She also draws pictures for many other storybooks and for greeting cards. Some of the dogs in her pictures look just like her pet terrier, Winnie!

Meet the Author

Virginia Mueller likes to do many things. She enjoys reading, playing the piano and organ, and visiting historic places. Most of all, she likes to write. Besides the storybooks about Monster, Mrs. Mueller has written many puzzle books for children.

Mrs. Mueller now lives in Wisconsin.

If I Had A Dinosaur

a song by Raffi

words by Raffi, D. Pike, and B. & B. Simpson

illustrated by Don Stuart

If I had a dinosaur,
Just think what we could do.
He could lift me off the floor
And take me to the zoo.

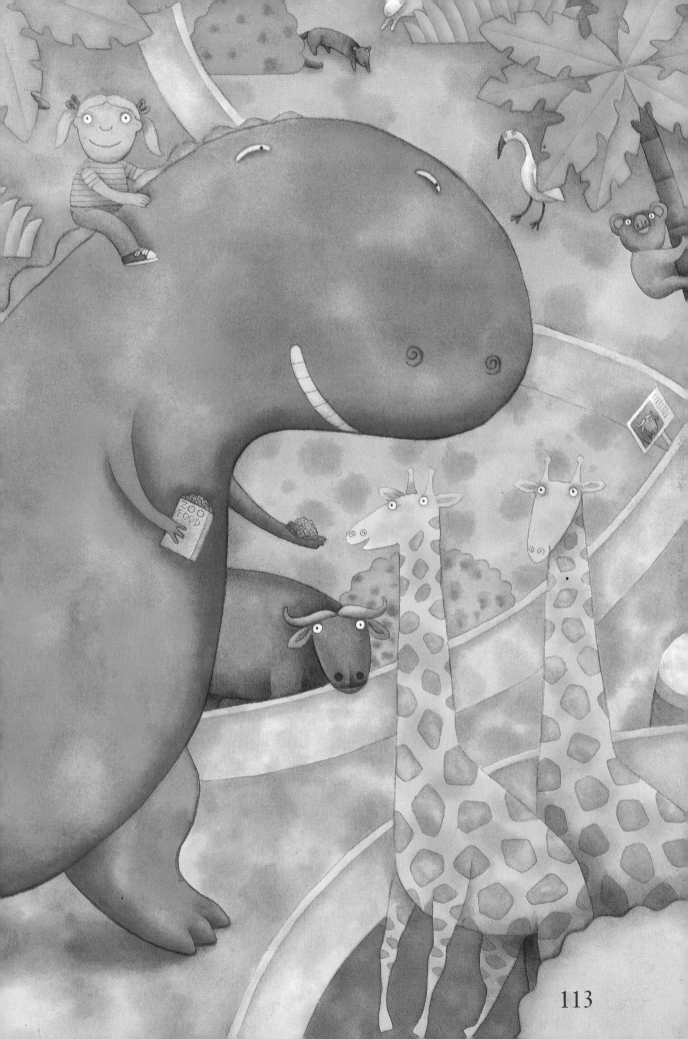

If I had a dinosaur,
Just think what we could see.
We could look inside the cloud
Above my balcony.

And if I had a dinosaur,
Just think where we could go.
All the way to Grandma's house
To play her piano.

117

If I Had A Dinosaur

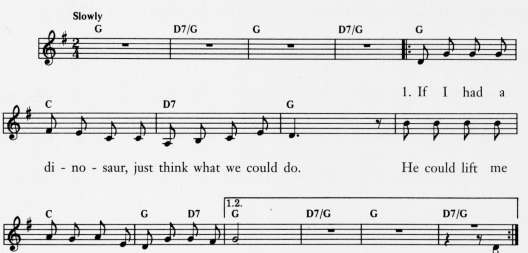

di-no-saur, just think what we could do. He could lift me

off the floor and take me to the zoo.

Meet the Songwriter

Raffi began writing songs in high school. One day he sang for a nursery school class. The children liked his songs so much that he went on to make a record album, *Singable Songs for the Very Young*. Today, Raffi is a very popular singer and songwriter.

A
Travel Poster

What other places could you go to if you were riding on top of a dinosaur? Make a travel poster about one of your ideas. Draw a picture of yourself riding your dinosaur. Next to your picture, write about some of the special places you would visit together. You might even want to add a map!

ARE THESE SPECIAL?

OODLES OF NOODLES

I love noodles. Give me oodles.
Make a mound up to the sun.
Noodles are my favorite foodles.
I eat noodles by the ton.

by Lucia and James L. Hymes, Jr.

BUGS

I am very fond of bugs.
I kiss them
And I give them hugs.

by Karla Kuskin

MUD

Mud is very nice to feel
    All squishy-squash between the toes!
I'd rather wade in wiggly mud
    Than smell a yellow rose.

Nobody else but the rosebush knows
How nice mud feels
    Between the toes.

by Polly Chase Boyden

SPECIAL! SPECIAL!

My Brown Bear Barney
by Dorothy Butler

The girl in this story takes her bear everywhere — even to the beach! As you read this story again, see if you can remember what else she takes with her.

I Need a Lunch Box
by Jeannette Caines

A boy wants his own special lunch box, even though he's not ready for school yet. Will his wish come true?

Three Happy Birthdays
by Judith Caseley

Read about how one family celebrates three special birthdays—with very surprising gifts!

READ ALL ABOUT IT!

Where Is It?

by Tana Hoban

A little white rabbit is looking for something special. Can you guess what it is?

Going Up!

by Peter Sis

Something is happening on the 12th floor. Find out why everyone in the elevator is going up, up, up!

A Place for Ben

by Jeanne Titherington

Ben finds a good place to be alone, but something is missing. What will happen to make Ben's place really special?

Acknowledgments

For each of the selections listed below, grateful acknowledgment is made for permission to excerpt and/or reprint original or copyrighted material, as follows:

Major Selections

"If I Had a Dinosaur," words and music by Raffi, D. Pike, B. & B. Simpson. Copyright © 1978 by Homeland Publishing, a division of Troubadour Records, Ltd. From *The Raffi Singable Songbook* (Crown/Random House Publishers). Reprinted by permission.

If I had a pig, by Mick Inkpen. Copyright © 1988 by Mick Inkpen. Reprinted by Macmillan Children's Books, a division of Macmillan Publishers, Ltd.

Monster Can't Sleep, text copyright © 1986 by Virginia Mueller. Illustrations copyright © 1986 by Lynn Munsinger. Originally published in hardcover by Albert Whitman and Company. All rights reserved. Used with permission.

"Raking Leaves" from *Punky Spends the Day* by Sally G. Ward. Copyright © 1989 by Sally G. Ward. Reprinted by permission of the publisher, Dutton Children's Books, a division of Penguin Books USA, Inc.

Sophie and Jack Help Out, text copyright © 1983 by Judy Taylor, illustrations copyright © 1983 by Susan Gantner. Reprinted by permission of Philomel Books, and The Bodley Head.

Poetry

"Bugs," from *Dogs and Dragons, Trees and Dreams* by Karla Kuskin. Originally published in *Alexander Soames: His Poems* by Karla Kuskin. Copyright © 1962 by Karla Kuskin. Reprinted by permission of Harper and Row, Publishers, Inc.

"Good Books, Good Times!" from *More Surprises* by Lee Bennett Hopkins. Copyright © 1985 by Lee Bennett Hopkins. Reprinted by permission of Curtis Brown, Ltd.

"Johnny," from *That Was Summer* by Marci Ridlon. Copyright © 1969 by Marci Ridlon and reprinted by her permission.

"Mud," by Polly Chase Boyden from *Child Life Magazine*. Copyright © 1930, 1958 by Rand McNally and Company. Extensive efforts to locate the rightsholder of this poem were unsuccessful. If the rightsholder sees this notice, he or she should contact the School Division Permissions Dept., Houghton Mifflin Co., One Beacon Street, Boston, MA 02108.

"My Dad and I," from *Runny Days, Sunny Days* by Aileen Fisher. Copyright © 1958 by Aileen Fisher; copyright renewed. Reprinted by permission of the author, who controls rights.

"My Teddy Bear," from *Rhymes About Us* by Marchette Chute. Copyright © 1974 by E. P. Dutton, Inc. Reprinted by permission of Mary Chute Smith.

"Oodles of Noodles," from *Oodles of Noodles* by Lucia and James L. Hymes, Jr. Copyright © 1964, Addison Wesley Publishing Co., Inc., Reading, Massachusetts. Reprinted with permission of the publisher.

"Wonderful Dinner," from *All About Me: Verses I Can Read* by Leland Jacobs. Copyright © 1971 by Leland B. Jacobs. Reprinted by permission of Leland B. Jacobs.

Read Along Books

The Read Along Books shown on pages 10, 68, 72, and 122 are available from Houghton Mifflin Company and are reprinted with permission from various publishers. Jacket artists for these books are listed below:

My Brown Bear Barney, by Dorothy Butler. Jacket art by Elizabeth Fuller, copyright © 1988 by Elizabeth Fuller.

Peanut Butter and Jelly, by Nadine Bernard Westcott. Jacket art by Nadine Bernard Westcott, copyright © 1987 by Nadine Bernard Westcott.

Additional Recommended Reading

Houghton Mifflin Company wishes to thank the following publishers for permission to reproduce their book covers on pages 68, 69, 122 and 123.

Clarion Books, a Houghton Mifflin Company: *Helping Out*, by George Ancona. Jacket photographs by George Ancona, copyright © 1985 by George Ancona.

Greenwillow Books, a division of William Morrow & Company, Inc.: *Busy Monday Morning*, by Janina Domanska. Jacket art by Janina Domanska, copyright © 1985 by Janina Domanska. *Going Up!* by Peter Sis. Jacket art by Peter Sis, copyright © 1989 by Peter Sis. *A Place for Ben*, by Jeanne Titherington. Jacket art by Jeanne Titherington, copyright © 1987 by Jeanne Titherington. *Three Happy Birthdays*, by Judith Caseley. Jacket art by Judith Caseley, copyright © 1989 by Judith Caseley.

Harcourt Brace Jovanovich, Publishers: *Growing Vegetable Soup*, by Lois Ehlert. Jacket art by Lois Ehlert, copyright © 1987 by Lois Ehlert.

Harper & Row, Publishers, Inc.: *I Need a Lunch Box*, by Jeannette Caines. Jacket art by Pat Cummings, copyright © 1988 by Pat Cummings.

Macmillan Publishing Company, Inc.: *Where Is It?* by Tana Hoban. Jacket art by Tana Hoban, copyright © 1974 by Tana Hoban.